The Magic Charm Chase

Adapted by Jenne Simon

from the teleplay by Anita Kapila

SCHOLASTIC INC.

Published by Scholastic Inc., *Publishers since 1920.* SCHOLASTIC and associated logos are trademarks and/or registered trademarks of Scholastic Inc.

ISBN 978-0-545-94302-4

10 9 8 7 6 5 4 3 2 1   16 17 18 19 20

Printed in the U.S.A.   40
First printing 2016
Book design by Erin McMahon and Becky James

It was a spell-tacularly busy day at Hazel's house. Hazel's mother was Charmville's Enchantress, and everyone in town needed her help!

"Too many spells, too little time," she told Hazel as she ran off to cure a frog with hiccups.

The Enchantress's to-do list was getting bigger by the second!
Hazel wanted to help her mom.

"I'll just make a copy of this list and go see Posie and Lavender,"
she said. "To the Charmhouse!"

Hazel's best friends, Lavender and Posie, met her at the Charmhouse.

"We'd love to help you," said Lavender.

"But this list is going to take us forever," added Posie.

"Maybe with a *normal* wand," Hazel said with a twinkle in her eye.

Lavender and Posie knew that look—Hazel had a plan!
She wanted to supercharge her wand.
"We'll be finished with this list in no time!" she said.
"Sparkle up, Charmers! We've got work to do."

Hocum, locum, zippidy-zong!
Power up my wand extra-strong!

Hazel chanted the magic words.

Soon sparks were flying around the Charmhouse.

"Looks like the spell worked," said Lavender.

But then Hazel's wand began to spin and splutter and smoke.
"Snapdragons!" cried Hazel. "I think I broke my wand!"
The girls used their magic mirror to go onto Spellipedia.
They looked up how to fix the wand.

The Charmers needed three ingredients: fairy dust from Mount Sparklemore, a giant's toenails, and sparkles from a unicorn's horn.

"You have to touch a unicorn before it reveals itself," read Hazel.

"And we can't use our wands to collect ingredients," added Lavender.

It wasn't going to be easy. But the Little Charmers were determined to get Hazel's magic back.

It took the girls hours to get to Mount Sparklemore. Now all they had to do was scoop up some fairy dust.

But every time Hazel took a step toward the mountain, a huge fairy mushroom popped up to block her path.

"They're here to protect Mount Sparklemore," said Posie as she bounced on top of a mushroom cap.

All that bouncing gave Hazel an idea.

"Follow me, Charmers!" she said. "In five, four, three, two, one . . ."

The girls took a step together, and a mushroom launched them up, up, up into the air!

Soon they were bouncing all the way to the top of Mount Sparklemore.

They sprinkled some fairy dust on Hazel's wand, and then set off to find a giant.

Luckily, Hazel knew where one lived. But when the girls knocked on his door, a cranky voice told them to go away.

"You are one grumpy giant," Posie said.

"You'd be grumpy, too, if you couldn't sleep," he boomed as he slammed the door.

That gave Posie an idea. She picked up her flute and began to play a lullaby.

Soon the giant was yawning and stretching and heading for bed.

The Little Charmers could sneak inside!

As Peep sleep.

Now

She t's bed and tugged at his

giant so

"You as she twisted the smelly

sock in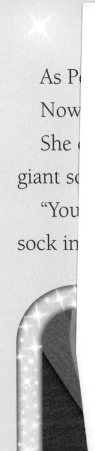

Hazel lassoed the giant's big toe, climbed up the sock rope, and snipped a bit of the giant's toenail. It was dirty work, but someone had to do it.

Once the deed was done, it was time to get out of there before the big grump woke up.

Two ingredients found, only one to go!

Next, the Little Charmers had to find a unicorn in the Forest of Thorns and Dragon Lilies. The flowers were pretty, but it was very prickly work.

"This is one fashion-unfriendly forest," said Lavender as she snagged her sleeve on a thorn for the millionth time.

The girls looked and looked, but they didn't see a unicorn anywhere! The shy creatures weren't hiding under dragon lily petals or in the forest's thorny brambles.

Hazel yawned. "A magic quest without magic powers sure is exhausting!"

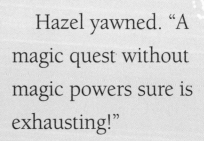

"You should stay here and rest," said Posie.

"We can look for the unicorn," added Lavender.

"Thanks!" Hazel said as she sat down. "I'll come help in a bit, I promise."

What Hazel needed was a nap. But no matter how she twisted and turned, she couldn't seem to get comfortable.

"It feels like my head is on something!" she said.

And when she looked up, she discovered what it was . . .

"Charmazing!" said Hazel.
"A unicorn! You're beautiful!"
The unicorn was soft like
clouds or puppies. It let
Hazel gather some sparkles
from its horn.

Now it was time to fix
Hazel's wand!

Hocum, locum, zippidy-zond! Ingredients combine and fix my wand!

In a flash of light, Hazel's wand found its magic! She shot a sparkle into the air to call her friends. She couldn't wait to introduce them to her new unicorn friend.

But when Posie and Lavender returned, the unicorn had vanished!

Back at home, Hazel told her parents all about her day and her magical new friend.

"I'm so lucky I got to see a unicorn," she sighed.

"You really are," said her mother. "That is very special magic."

"Special enough to help with your to-do list?" Hazel asked.

"I hope so," said her mom. "It looks like it just got bigger." She took a closer look. "Curing hiccups? Not that poor frog again!"

Hazel's dad winked. "Not—*hic*—this—*hic*—time!"

Hazel laughed. A little magic could solve the trickiest—and *hic*-iest—of problems!